This book belongs to

.....................

Front endpapers by Hannah Shepard aged 8 (left) and Liam Tye aged 7 (right)
Back endpapers by and Banita Gill aged 10 (left) and Ryan Haigh aged 8 (right)

Thank you to Stephen Freeman Primary School, Didcot for all their help with the endpapers—K.P.

For Ola—K.P.

## OXFORD
### UNIVERSITY PRESS

Great Clarendon Street, Oxford OX2 6DP

Oxford University Press is a department of the University of Oxford.
It furthers the University's objective of excellence in research, scholarship,
and education by publishing worldwide in

Oxford  New York

Auckland  Cape Town  Dar es Salaam  Hong Kong  Karachi
Kuala Lumpur  Madrid  Melbourne  Mexico City  Nairobi
New Delhi  Shanghai  Taipei  Toronto

With offices in
Argentina  Austria  Brazil  Chile  Czech Republic  France  Greece
Guatemala  Hungary  Italy  Japan  Poland  Portugal  Singapore
South Korea  Switzerland  Thailand  Turkey  Ukraine  Vietnam

© Text copyright Oxford University Press 2014
© Illustrations copyright Korky Paul 1987, 1996, 1997, 2002,
2005, 2006, 2007, 2009, 2010, 2011, 2012, 2013, 2014
Based on books in the 'Winnie the Witch' series by Valerie Thomas and Korky Paul
The moral rights of the author and artist have been asserted

Database right Oxford University Press (maker)

First published 2014

British Library Cataloguing in Publication Data available

ISBN: 978-0-19273833-2 (paperback)

2 4 6 8 10 9 7 5 3 1

Printed in Singapore

Paper used in the production of this book is a natural, recyclable product made
from wood grown in sustainable forests. The manufacturing process conforms
to the environmental regulations of the country of origin

This is Korky Paul who draws the Winnie pictures.
Can you find him inside this book?

www.korkypaul.com

Valerie Thomas and Korky Paul

# What Would You Do in Winnie's World?

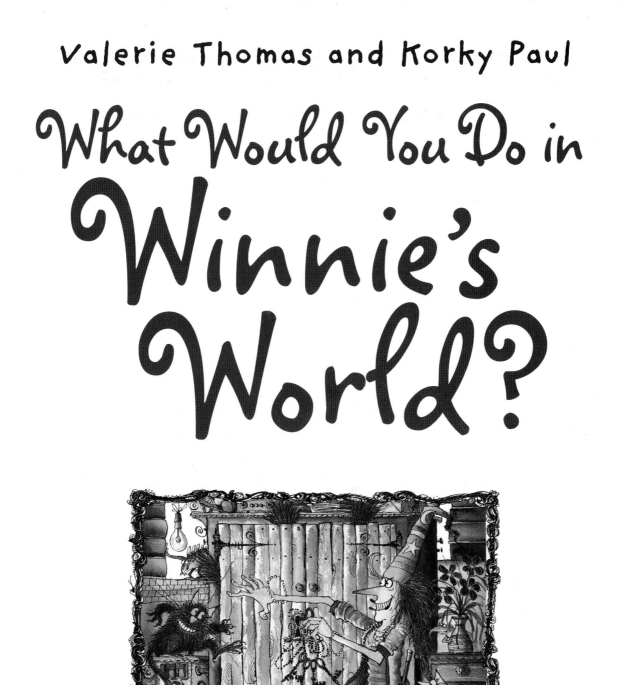

OXFORD
UNIVERSITY PRESS

Winnie the Witch and Wilbur
live in a big black house.

Where would you like to live
in Winnie's world?

Can you find
someone shaking a
fist and a lady
in a window?

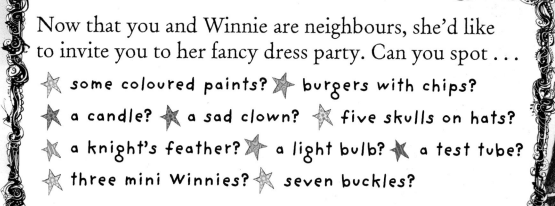

Now that you and Winnie are neighbours, she'd like to invite you to her fancy dress party. Can you spot . . .

⭐ some coloured paints? ⭐ burgers with chips?

⭐ a candle? ⭐ a sad clown? ⭐ five skulls on hats?

⭐ a knight's feather? ⭐ a light bulb? ⭐ a test tube?

⭐ three mini Winnies? ⭐ seven buckles?

# Winnie travels everywhere by broomstick.

How would you get around in Winnie's world?

Can you find three giant wands and a spare tyre?

Winnie loves her big
black cat Wilbur.

Which Wilbur is your
favourite today?

Can you find two Wilburs that are exactly the same?

Once Winnie waved her magic wand to turn a pumpkin into a helicopter.

If you had a magic wand what would you turn these things into?

What would you turn me into?

Look! Winnie has turned her big black house into a colourful one. If you look carefully, can you spot . . .

- ★ a red and a blue tap?
- ★ a pair of purple pants?
- ★ two yellow chimneys each with two yellow chimney pots?
- ★ two golden birds?
- ★ three green plants in pots?
- ★ a blue mug?  ★ some red pipes?
- ★ a white doorknob? ★ two purple bottles? ★ a blue ladder?

# Winnie is always bumping into people!

## Who would you like to meet in Winnie's world?

# Wilbur is not the only animal in Winnie's world.

## What kind of creature would you choose as a pet?

There are dinosaurs galore in Winnie's world. But can you spot . . .
⭐ a watch? ⭐ a dinosaur in a bottle?
⭐ a pair of flip flops? ⭐ 10 blue shoes? ⭐ a briefcase? ⭐ two earrings? ⭐ a spotty hatband?
⭐ two tongues sticking out?
⭐ a foot on a tube of paint?
⭐ a feather that isn't on a bird?

# Where would you go in Winnie's world?

And who would you take with you?

# There's always time for fun in Winnie's world!

What would *you* most like to do for a perfect day
with Winnie and Wilbur?

# What happens next in Winnie's world?

Use these picture sequences to start your own stories!

## An underwater adventure

## A night-time visitor

## A journey into space

## A new computer

## A dinosaur experience

## A flying carpet

## A winter's day

## A pirate voyage